蛇
Snake

龍
Dragon

馬
Horse

兔
Rabbit

羊
Sheep

For nearly 5,000 years, the Chinese culture has organized time in cycles of twelve years. This Eastern calendar is based upon the movement of the moon (as compared to the Western calendar which follows the sun's path). The zodiac circle symbolizes how animals, which have unique qualities, represent each year. Therefore, if you are born in a particular year, then you share the personality of that animal. Now people worldwide celebrate this fifteen-day festival in the early spring and enjoy the start of another Chinese New Year.

虎
Tiger

猴
Monkey

牛
Ox

雞
Rooster

鼠
Rat

狗
Dog

豬
Pig

To my Aunt Lily, Esther, Madeline, and Margie:
your hospitality, leadership, and generosity will
always inspire me.
—O.C.

For my Dad whose constant love, support, and
caring advice have always guided me down the
right tracks.
—J.W.

immedium

Immedium, Inc.
P.O. Box 31846
San Francisco, CA 94131
www.immedium.com

First hardcover edition published 2013.

Edited by Don Menn
Book design by Erica Loh Jones
Calligraphy by Lucy Chu

Printed in Malaysia
10 9 8 7 6 5 4 3 2 1

Library of Congress Cataloging-in-Publication Data

Chin, Oliver Clyde, 1969-
The year of the snake : tales from the Chinese zodiac / by Oliver Chin ; illustrated by Jennifer Wood.
-- 1st hardcover ed.
p. cm.
Summary: Suzie the snake befriends a girl named Lily, as well as some other animals of the Chinese lunar calendar, and demonstrates the value of being resourceful. Lists the birth years and characteristics of individuals born in the Chinese Year of the Snake.
ISBN 978-1-59702-038-1 (hardcover)
[1. Snakes--Fiction. 2. Resourcefulness--Fiction. 3. Animals--Fiction. 4. Astrology, Chinese--Fiction.] I. Wood, Jennifer, ill. II. Title.
PZ7.C44235Yeu 2013
[E]--dc23

2012015095

ISBN 978-1359702-038-1

Tales from the Chinese Zodiac

Written by Oliver Chin
Illustrated by Jennifer Wood

immedium
www.immedium.com
San Francisco. CA

One bright morning, a mother and father snake awoke from their winter's nap and started a family in their den underground. Delighted by all their squirmy snakelets, the parents named their last baby Suzie.

Suzie slithered about the nest with her
older brothers and sister. Mama said,
"Come with us outside to bask in the sun."
So Suzie tagged along.

Once at the surface, she saw a dazzling
and colorful world.

Other animals were surprised by a snake in the grass. "Don't tread on me!" Papa warned.

But Suzie enjoyed the sunlight. Overhead a dragon soared. Watching her relative, she thought, **"I wonder what it's like up there."**

But Mama advised her, "Always remember your place. Hug the earth and stick with your own kind."

Papa added, "Yes, it's time for us to return home and go to sleep."

But Suzie still wanted to smell everything the world had to offer and to view life from on high. So uncoiling from her tightly knit family, she silently slipped away from the snake pit.

Though she didn't have arms or legs, Suzie could twist her body in many directions. Copying a swinging monkey, she trailed it to a beautiful garden. Hanging from a fruit tree, Suzie spied a girl walking by.

Careful not to startle her, the serpent warmly introduced herself,

"*HISS*...hello!
My name is Suzie."

The girl replied,
"Good morning. I'm Lily."
They shared a sweet snack and instantly became friends.

Lily invited Suzie to her grandparent's house. But Grandpa Yeh Yeh whispered, "Didn't we tell you not trust anyone with a forked tongue?"

Grandma Nin Nin shivered, "All our other guests leave their shoes by the door."

Suzie was disappointed by this cold reception.

But just then she noticed a rat taking some cheese. As she zipped after it, Suzie told Lily, **"Follow me and hold onto my tail!"**

Lily poked her like
a stick into the hole.
Finally she pulled out
Suzie who nabbed the rat.

"That's some trick!" exclaimed Yeh Yeh.

Nin Nin prodded, "Honey, take her outside – maybe she can help you finish your chores."

Leaving the house, Suzie was eager to meet the neighbors. Lily's first job was to walk the dog, but she had forgotten to bring a leash.

But Suzie promptly latched onto the dog's collar, and away they went.

Soon they saw a rooster perched atop the chicken coop. "I flew up here," he clucked nervously. "But I'm afraid to come down by myself."

Lily stretched her hands but couldn't reach the bird.

"The rooster is our alarm clock every morning," explained Lily. "If he doesn't get a good night's rest in the henhouse, then we will all oversleep."

Suzie tapped her head with her tail and out came an idea.

Lily held onto her pal's tail again and tossed her into the air. The snake's fangs grabbed onto the roof. Suzie became a tightrope! Then the relieved rooster tiptoed across into Lily's waiting arms.

The group continued along and heard a cry from the pigpen. "Help!" the pig squealed. "I'm stuck in the mud."

"Pitch me in," proposed Suzie.

The pig clutched onto the scaly lifeline and everyone tugged her out.

Nearby Lily noticed the sheep's fence needed repair. **"I can pen the sheep in, while you fix it,"** suggested Suzie.

While the snake acted like a rail, Lily hammered the wood post back in.

Next, Lily had to plow the fields with the ox.
"The harness has frayed," sighed Lily.
"What shall we do?"

But Suzie volunteered to knot the
yoke in place. She gritted her teeth
as the team dug row after row.

Finally, the pair had to bring the horse back to the barn. The two friends shared the same thought.

So in the corral, Lily used Suzie as a rope to lasso the horse.

The girls were happy at the results of their hard day's work.

Lily's grandparents grudgingly admitted that Suzie had been handier than they had expected.

But just then, the square's warning bell rang.

A wild tiger had been spotted nearby.
"Everyone, run home!" cried Nin Nin.
Townsfolk hastily boarded up their
windows and locked their doors.
But Suzie convinced Lily that
they could lend a hand.

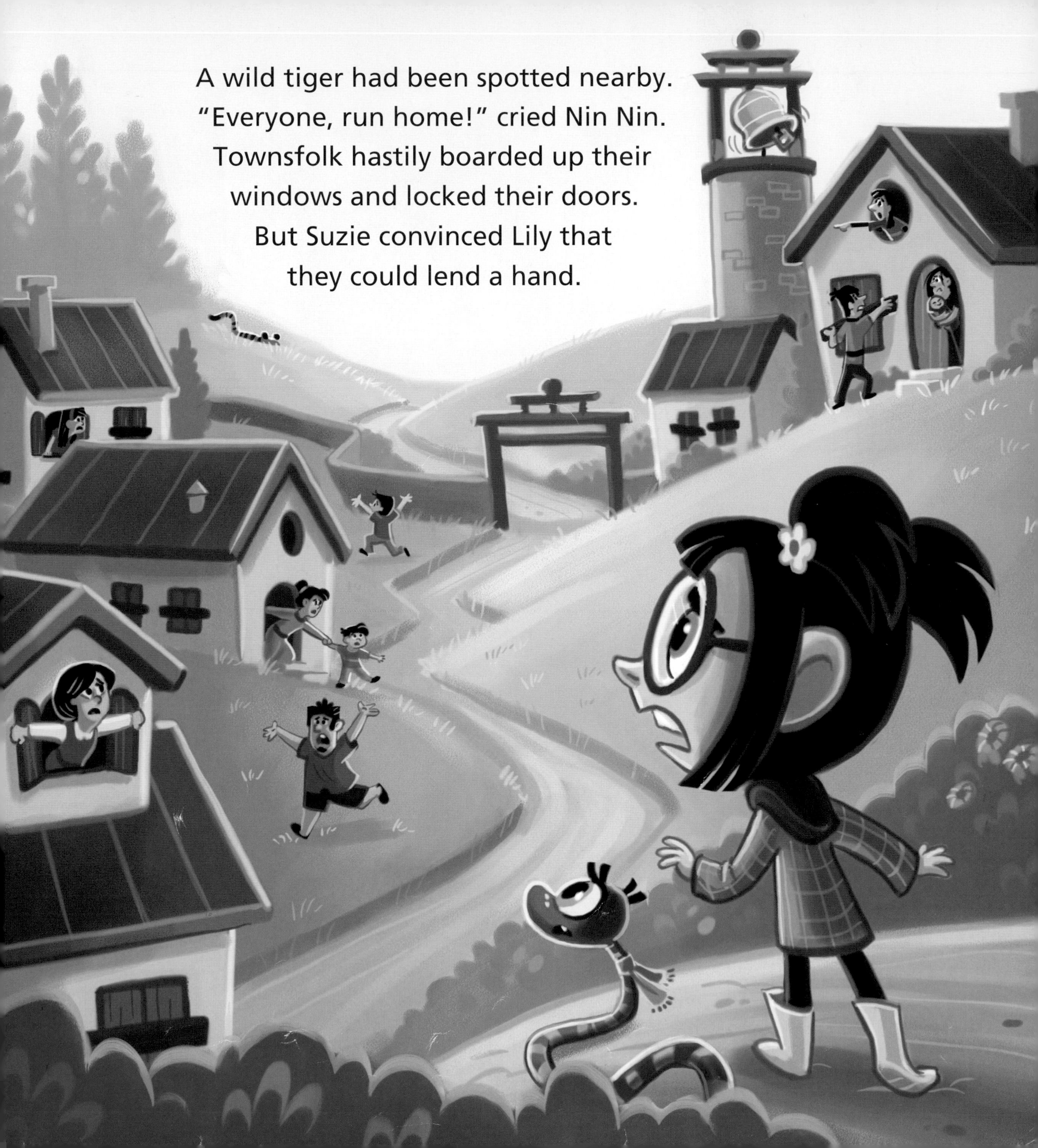

Itching for action,
the girls headed to the
beginning of the main
street. There Suzie
formed a loop. Lily
carefully placed Suzie
in the dirt, and hid in
the bushes.

Along came the tiger,
racing down the path.

"HISS!" shouted Suzie.
The trap was sprung!

The snake snared the feet of the big cat,
who roared in surprise. However,
the tiger was much different from
what the girls had imagined.

"I'm fleeing from a fire-breathing monster," the tiger gasped. "The mad beast is coming this way!"

In the distance, smoke and flames shot across the sky. Strangely, Suzie felt like she was on fire, too!

"Ow! I have a big itch!" Suzie cried.

Luckily, Mama and Papa snake appeared. "We missed you!"

They hugged their daughter and told her what to do. So Suzie rubbed her tingling skin against a rock, back and forth.

When she was done,
Suzie sparkled like new,
much to Lily's delight.
Quickly they hatched
a plan to deal with the
approaching dragon.

The snake
climbed a tree,
went out on a limb,
and lay in wait.

At last the dragon landed. But it stopped in its tracks to examine something very odd.

"What kind of animal is this?" it snorted.
It was a snakeskin.

Suddenly Suzie jumped from the branches,
"HISS!"

The snake wrapped herself tightly around her big cousin's snout. Shocked, it lifted off like a rocket.

But squeezing hard, Suzie soon stopped the dragon's fire.

This calmed the creature and it glided back down.

Along the way, Suzie relaxed her grip.

"Thanks for helping me," the dragon explained. "I had an uncontrollable case of the hiccups!"

"You're welcome," replied Suzie, who appreciated the sizzling ride.

Once on the ground, Suzie received a warm welcome. People admired how Suzie didn't blink in the face of danger, and Lily knew her buddy had won over many hearts.

Yeh Yeh and Nin Nin treasured Suzie's visits like she was their own granddaughter.

Likewise, Mama and Papa snake were kind hosts to Lily and enjoyed introducing her to their unusual ways.

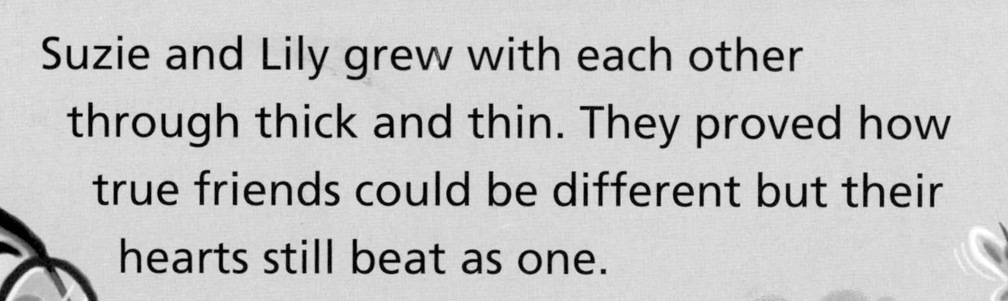

Suzie and Lily grew with each other through thick and thin. They proved how true friends could be different but their hearts still beat as one.

Through life's twists and turns, Lily and Suzie scaled many peaks.

And everyone agreed that this was a sensational Year of the Snake.

Snake

1917, 1929, 1941, 1953, 1965, 1977, 1989, 2001, 2013, 2025

People born in the Year of the Snake seem to warm slowly and savor their leisure. Though they appear slippery and secretive, they can be steely and decisive. But proving both sensitive and flexible, snakes emerge as truly charming and clever friends.